# Scamp's New Home

*by*

Joey Elliott

Scamp took a deep breath, then closed his ears to keep water out. Down he dove, moving his sleek, brown body in waves, pumping his webbed hind feet up and down to propel him. Light fell through streamers of kelp. Small fish darted about, stirring bits of sand and seaweed. Scamp followed a thick ribbon of kelp down to the hold-fast at its base. There he came upon a bed of clams.

At once, he pulled out the loose skin below his arm to form a sort of pocket. Into the fold he slipped three fat clams. Then he grabbed a rock in his free hand and turned to swim for the surface. But he spotted a purple sea urchin just outside the edge of the kelp forest. Tucking the rock under his other arm, he grabbed the spiny urchin. In a graceful curve of bubbles, he rose toward the surface again.

Whoo-o-osh! The great shadow of a shark slid by overhead. Scamp could see the gleam of its sharp, white teeth. Quickly, he twisted back toward the kelp to hide. But after nearly three minutes underwater, his lungs were bursting. He had to go up! Pumping his feet hard, he shot toward the surface. There, from the safety of the kelp, he watched the shark's fin moving away.

Scamp flipped onto his back. He placed the rock, the clams and the urchin on his belly. He lifted a clam, smashing it down onto the rock. The shell cracked, and he sucked out the soft food within.

Scamp loved shellfish—mussels, clams, and snails—but the spiny, purple urchin was his favorite. There were many in this forest of giant kelp. They fed on the green plants. And Scamp fed on the urchins. In this way, everything remained in balance. If the urchins became too plentiful, they could destroy the kelp. And Scamp needed the kelp for protection. Big animals, like killer whales and sharks, stayed clear of the kelp beds where they might become entangled and drown.

Scamp combed all the crumbs and bits of clam from his belly with his small, padded hands. Finally, he rolled like a corkscrew, turning over and over to rinse. He had to keep his fur clean. Even a speck of dirt could let the icy water in. An otter with bad habits would soon freeze.

He thought for a moment about the shark. He shivered. "I am alone too much," he sighed. "When I am alone, I daydream. In fact, I am lonely."

"Ho, Scamp," called a voice from shore. Turning his head, Scamp spotted Sage, the mountain goat. "Come over here," called Sage. "For I am unlikely to come out there."

"Just a goat, who cannot float," sang Scamp, who loved to rhyme. And he swam quickly on his back, using first one webbed foot, then the other, to propel him. "What's new? I've missed you!"

Sage laughed. "I've just returned from the high cliffs to the north," he replied. "The snow is still deep, so I could not find much food. But Scamp, I have news!"

"What news?" asked Scamp, eagerly. "Is it fine news? Is it my news?" And Scamp did a backflip dive, just for fun.

Sage chuckled. "What will I do when there are ten like you," sighed Sage. "Making rhymes and splashing me."

"Ten?" asked Scamp, puzzled. "Like me?" Just then, a small, white form darted across the snow.

"Frolic," called Scamp. "How nice. Watch the ice!" For the spring thaw made the edges of the bank slippery. But the snowshoe hare stopped short of the edge.

"Hello," said Frolic, breathlessly. "I'm glad to see you two. I've run here to escape from a lynx and a wolf. This morning everyone in Dry Bay wants snowshoe hare for breakfast."

"Not me," said Scamp and Sage in unison.

"You are just in time to hear Sage's news," said Scamp, worried that Sage had forgotten.

"What news?" asked Frolic, grooming her long ears.

"News of more sea otters," said Sage. "Just like you, Scamp. I saw them from the cliffs."

"Oh, where?" cried Scamp. For he had not seen any other sea otters for a very long time.

"You must go north from the opening of the Alsek River," Sage replied. "I think you must swim for several days."

"Oh, no, Scamp," objected Frolic. "It could be dangerous. If you leave your kelp, how will you find food?"

"And I have seen killer whales off the coast," said Sage. "I have seen their black and white markings."

“Oh, dear,” fretted Scamp. “Killer whales sometimes eat sea otters. Though perhaps the new otters live near another kelp forest.”

“I couldn’t see,” said Sage. “It was too far. Even for me.”

“Oh dear, oh dear,” worried Frolic. But Sage just trotted away toward the cliffs.

That night, Scamp thought and thought. He was safely wrapped in two ribbons of kelp, to keep him from drifting. The bay was silent in the deep blue twilight. Far away, the northern lights shifted and danced, like a curtain of pale light. All was peaceful. All but Scamp.

“I remember otters,” he thought. “Long, long ago. I remember playing and diving with them. I remember my mother’s soft kisses and warm milk, and sleeping on her chest. I remember when she taught me to dive and to fish. Where did all those otters go?”

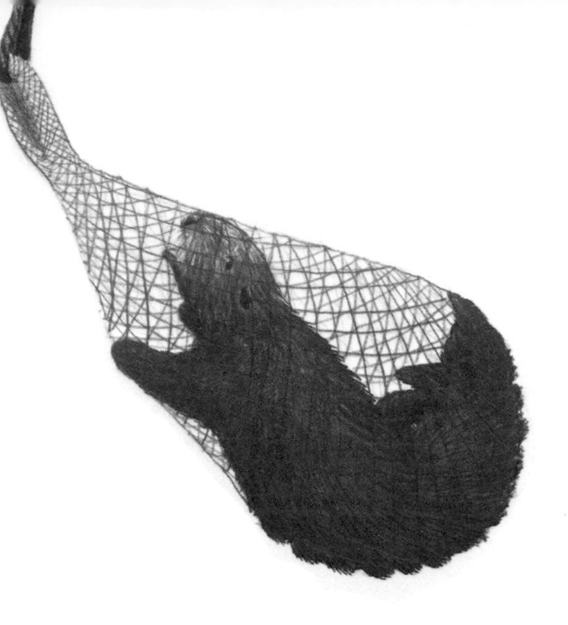

Dimly, Scamp recalled a day when he was caught by a strange webbing. He tried to free himself, to bite through the net. But soon he found himself dumped into a box, all alone. Through the walls he could hear a pup, crying mournfully. And he could hear the mother, answering. A steady, loud noise thrummed and thrummed.

After what seemed like forever, the otters' voices began to disappear. Scamp would hear a loud splash, and another otter's voice would be gone. Then Scamp's box bumped open. Out he was dumped, into the water near Dry Bay. That same night, a huge storm had blown in from the sea. The frightened otters had been tossed in all directions. The raging storm had swallowed their cries. By morning, the bay was calm. But Scamp had found himself alone. He had not seen another otter since that day.

"The trip may be dangerous," he thought. "But I have been lonely. I have a feeling otters belong with otters. If it is so, then I must go." And having decided, Scamp fell asleep at last.

At daybreak, Scamp began diving for food. When he had eaten all he could, he cleaned and combed his fur. With a last look at Dry Bay, he began swimming north.

As he swam, Scamp kept alert for danger. Once, he spotted a gray whale. But Scamp knew a gray whale would never attack a sea otter. Once, he saw the water rippling with many smooth, brown bodies. He swam even faster, hoping to see whiskered, golden faces like his own. But it was only sea lions, rolling in the waves near shore.

On and on he swam. When he could find kelp, to keep him from drifting into the rocks, he rested.

On the third morning, Scamp was rounding a bend in the rocky coast when he spotted a black speck in the sky, circling high above. At first, he thought the speck was a seagull. But as it flew lower, in big, looping circles, it grew larger.

Then, two things happened, very fast. Scamp heard the terrified cry of a sea otter. It seemed to be coming from just beyond the crest of a tall wave. And, looking up, Scamp realized that the speck circling overhead was a bald eagle.

An eagle will rarely go after an adult sea otter. But the frightened squeals of the otter pup stirred a memory. "Sea otter pups cannot dive," Scamp thought. "They bob on the surface like corks. That eagle wants the pup!" Swiftly, Scamp swam toward the cry.

Just then, an answering call began. It was the mother, calling her pup. She had been on a long dive, searching for food while her pup slept. But the pup must have drifted from his safe bed of kelp. Now the eagle was swooping down. Soon he would grab the pup and carry him off into the sky.

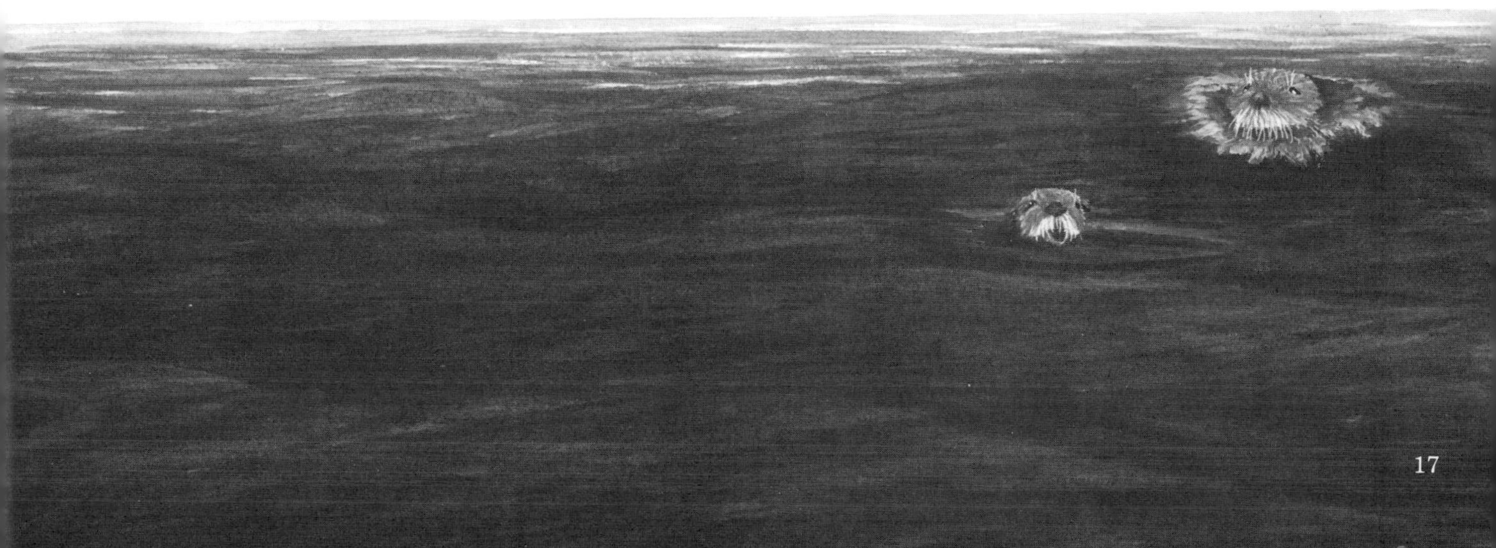

"Help, help," squealed the pup.

"I'm coming," called the mother, and she sped toward her baby. But the eagle dropped like a stone. Down, down he came, falling toward the pup. The pup squealed and squealed. Scamp splashed to distract the eagle and slow his fall. The eagle turned his fierce, yellow eyes toward Scamp. The mother otter reached her pup just in time. She grabbed him, tucked him under an arm, and dove. Scamp dove, too. The eagle skimmed the top of the waves, fanned his wings, and screamed with anger. He rose from the water with empty claws.

Soon the eagle was just a speck again. Then he was gone. Scamp shivered with relief. He watched as the anxious mother combed and fluffed her pup's fur. She fondled the baby, and kissed him on his head.

A splashing sound drew Scamp's attention. Nearby, playing and frisking and dunking each other, was a whole pod of male otters. Scamp hurried to join them. A young male surfaced in a bright spray of water.

"Good day," greeted the otter. "Want to play? Want to stay?"

Scamp was overjoyed. Another rhymer!

"Scamp is my name," he said. "I'd love a game." And the two otters tumbled and somersaulted under the fine morning sky.

After a while they hunted, finding small clams and even a tiny crab. Scamp noticed that the kelp fronds were thin and ragged. There were few urchins. He asked his new friend, Dodger, about it. Dodger told Scamp that a little kelp was better than no kelp. But Scamp worried.

That night, Scamp dozed near the other otters. Because the kelp was thin, it was difficult to remain together. Now and then Scamp drifted from the group. Then he would have to swim back. By morning, he was weary. But he ate, and groomed, and felt better. He began to feel this must be his new home. He romped and tussled with Dodger. Then he lay back to clean his fur again. Lifting his head, he glanced toward the pod of females, floating with their pups in the sunshine.

Something was wrong. Several large waves were not moving in a smooth line with the others. In fact, they seemed to be coming straight toward the females. Then he spotted the black and white markings that could be so deadly.

"Swim for kelp," he yelled. "Swim for shore!"

The females began calling their pups. The water was churning with motion. Some otters dove to escape. Others raced to hide among the shreds of kelp. Dodger headed for shore. But Scamp stayed near the females. Two mothers were in trouble! If they were alone, they might play dead. But their pups would not stay quiet. So the mothers tucked the babies under their arms and dove. Each time, they rose closer to the kelp. But each time, the whales were closer, too.

One pair of otters reached the kelp. But one mother and her pup never surfaced again.

"Those poor otters," said Scamp. "I was lucky. But what about next time? That was very close."

"Too close," agreed Dodger, surfacing nearby. "We must find another home."

"I swam such a long way," said Scamp, sadly. "I thought this would be my new home."

"But this is not a safe home," said an older otter. "A big storm would ground us. There is not enough kelp to smooth the waves. There are not enough strands for anchors. And there is not enough food."

“We need a place with a shore where we can climb out to dry and fluff our fur,” said Dodger.

“A place with plenty of kelp,” said another.

“A place with plenty of urchins,” said a third. “And crabs, and clams, and starfish,” he added wistfully.

“I don’t like starfish,” whispered Dodger.

“But I know a place,” exclaimed Scamp. “I know a place exactly like that!”

“Where?” chorused the otters.

“Follow me,” said Scamp. “I’ll take you to a new home. A fine home.”

And one by one, the sea otters began to follow. First the male pod, and then at a distance, the females and their pups. They made quite a ripple, moving along the shoreline.

Many days later, Beezle, the moose calf, was standing in the shallow water in Dry Bay. Nearby was Sage. Beezle stared out over the water.

"Well," said Sage, "Are you going for a swim, Beezle, or not?"

"I see something," said Beezle. "Come and look."

Sage came closer. "It looks like several somethings," said Sage. "Several somethings we know quite well."

A small, white ball of fluff bounded over to join them.

"Hello, Frolic," said Sage. "Do you see who is coming?"

"Scamp," piped Frolic, joyfully. "Scamp is home!"

And indeed it was Scamp, proudly leading the two pods of otters to his kelp forest in the waters of Dry Bay. Beezle and Sage watched in silence as the otters ducked and dived. They rode the rollercoaster waves gleefully. They tossed balls of seaweed into the air, and caught them. They splashed and tumbled in the safety of the kelp. The bay sparkled and danced with light.

"Oh, Scamp," said Frolic happily. "Welcome home!"

*To the sea otters of Prince William Sound*

*The author gratefully acknowledges the technical assistance of Lowell Suring, of the Department of Wildlife and Fisheries in Alaska, and Dr. Charles Handley of The Smithsonian Institution.*

Points of Interest in This Book

p. 1. kelp "holdfast"; clams
p. 3. blue shark
p. 5. surf scoters
p. 6. mountain goat; snowshoe hare
pp. 12–13. Note: At one time, sea otters were hunted along coastal Alaska until finally there were no more. The Department of Wildlife and Fisheries caught otters near the Aleutian Islands and brought them to coastal Alaska in crates aboard boats. Even now, otters are finding new homes along Alaskan shores.
p. 13. tufted puffins
p. 14. gray whale
p. 15. sea lions
p. 16. bald eagle
p. 19. kelp greenlings
Note: The male and female of this species of fish have very different coloring.
p. 21. "pod" or "raft": a group of otters; male and female pods stay apart
p. 24. killer whales, or orcas
Note: In kelp beds, these rarely threaten otters.

 Corporation, 165 Water Street, Norwalk, CT 06856. Manufactured by Horowitz/Rae Book Manufacturers, Inc. Designed by Judy Oliver, Oliver and Lake Design Associates. First edition 10 9 8 7 6 5 4 3 2 1.

Library of Congress Cataloging-in-Publications Data
Elliott, Joey Scamp's New Home
Summary: A lonely sea otter finds other sea otters and brings them to his home near the mouth of the Alsek River in Alaska.
1. Sea otter—juvenile literature [1. Sea otter]
1. Elliott, Joey. 11. Title.
ISBN: 0-924483-16-4